KATZ KAN!!!

A Katz Perspective

By

T.T. Daniels

ISBN: 978-1-7385650-0-9 (Print)
ISBN: 978-1-7385650-1-6 (Ebook)
ISBN: 978-1-7385650-2-3 (Audiobook)

Any references to historical events, real people, or real places are coincidental; names, characters, and places are products of the author's imagination.

Front cover image by Beluga Tequila.

Mindjewels Publishing

First printing edition 2024.

DEDICATION

This book is dedicated to Mittens Goo, whose unwavering companionship fills my days with warmth and joy.

INTRODUCTION

This book is tailor-made for the dreamers, the adventurers, and believers in the power of imagination. Step into a world where imagination knows no bounds, where the lines between reality and fantasy blur into a tapestry of wonder and intrigue.

If you've ever felt the tug of curiosity, or the spark of wonder igniting within you, then rest assured, this book is your ticket to an unforgettable experience. Katz Kan!! A Katz Perspective, is the key to a thrilling escapade through whimsical wonderment, where the hidden depths of these enchanting worlds are revealed. With a passion for igniting imaginations, I am uniquely positioned to guide you through this immersive adventure.

Through captivating prose, vivid imagery, vibrant characters, unexpected twists and spellbinding narratives, you will be transported to a realm where anything is possible. Together, we will unravel the mysteries of Catlantis, uncovering the profound truths that lie dormant beneath its surface.

Join me on this odyssey of discovery, where each page is a portal to new realms of possibility and wonder. Let us unlock the door to boundless creativity and embark on a journey that will leave an indelible mark on your soul.

When words pour, imaginations soar, desire is the key, your mind is the door.

TABLE OF CONTENTS

CHAPTER 1

NEWS BULLETIN!!!! (Television News Reader)

"The danger is approaching the South West. Three cities have disappeared in as many minutes. We may not be on air much longer. Gather your families. Stay Safe. Do the best you can. Godspeed."

(Screen goes black)

Pete Katz shouts to his wife, "Candy Girl, we gotta get outta here, it's not safe for us here anymore. I've called the Goldsteins, my cousin in West Catlantis, the Silver-Katz, and NO RESPONSE. ANYWHERE. WE'RE OUT!!!"

"I'll get the Kitty Katz and meet you at the Winnebago, ASAP," Candy purrs from the kitchen. (The Kitty Katz, as Candy often affectionately referred to their three offspring, were twins Kyle, (known as Kool to his friends), Kiera (who her mother called Ki-Ki, which Kiera hated), and their oldest Pete Jnr (known as Junior Katz).

Candy reaches the top of the stairs, "You Kitty Katz got 9 minutes to get your stuff and haul your tails downstairs by the Winnie!!!" "But Mum...." said an agitated Kiera. "DO IT!!! Save all your energy for packing," said Candy as she moved gracefully yet quickly down the stairs.

(RADIO IN KITCHEN)

"There have been reports that the Catcavern area has all but disappeared. We fear the worst."

CHAPTER 2

Pete Katz waited anxiously for his family to join him in the Winnebago. He always enjoyed their family adventures. The memories of fun times teased his mind. However, this was no family adventure, it was an emergency.

Now the Kitty Katz were all grown, they didn't have too much time for family vacations. Adolescent pursuits and social media were now the top priority. Family time was confined to special occasions and dinner every Sunday.

Or one Sunday a month, if you worked away and had a good excuse, like Tony "Top" Katz. Pete's older brother and CEO of KatzScratch - Number One Supplier of scratching posts and high-end cat accessories in Catlantis for the last 30 years.

"What's up with these Katz???" Pete grows impatient and is eager to get a move on. He knows the roads out of town will be jam-packed and road blocked, which will only add to his anxiety.

Pete blows the horn... "Keep it down" purrs Candy, her fur unruffled, "That horn sounds like an elephant." Bending her neck around the banister, she shouts, "Are you Katz ready?"

"Yeah Mom," shouted two of three available voices in unison. "Coming now," said the missing voice. The Kitty Katz knew the drill, this was not the first time they had been given a "9 Minute Warning."

It all began when Pete Junior was a kitten. Pete Senior was a "cat about town," with his paw on the pulse. A paw in every pie, kind of cat, some would say. He knew a good deal when he heard one.

So, when he heard of some real estate going for an exceptionally reasonable price, he jumped in head first, fur flying.

These deals were like Catnip to Pete. Being in the "loop" Pete always got wind of the opportunities as they turned up. This was one that he could not refuse.

He remembers the morning of the move, everything was "Perfect." Three years later. "Candy Girl... We GOTTA move. We got like nine good minutes!!!"

This is what happens when buying real estate in Catlantis he thought. Ever since.... Was that even true? he wondered.

I'll really need to take some time to investigate that, he mused, making a mental note. Just then, he heard voices. The troops were on the move. Cases and personal effects were all aboard.

The Katz gang is now ready for the road. "Seatbelts on, we're on the move" shouts Pete. "Heading East?" asks Candy. Pete nods a slow yes, his whiskers twitching.

He knew what lay to the East. If the rumours were "true," they would be safe, thought Pete, as the Winnebago's powerful engine roared into action and it rolled majestically out of the garage.

Kiera Katz suddenly shouts out "One-minute Dad!!!" The brakes screeeeeech into action. Kiera jumps out of the Winnebago and rescues the sign that she had made for the family driveway in wood shop, a sign that she was very proud of, "The Katz Kattery."

The Katz family all laughed as Kyle said he was, "Amazed that Kiera had managed to remember anything that wasn't connected to her phone."

Just the mood lightener they all needed.

CHAPTER 3

It was not very often that the Katz got to spend time with each other. A "9-minute warning" always raised that feeling of cohesion between them.

They knew when it was time to pull together. The Kitty Katz were quiet and on their "apps," and who knows whatever else, in the back.

Pete and Candy were glad for the silence as they studied the Winnebago's satellite navigation.

"I reckon 500 miles East should keep us out of harm's reach, for now," said Pete.

"Hmmmmm," purred Candy. "That may keep us out of the danger beneath us, but what about......."

"What choice have we got Candy?" said Pete, trying to be the voice of logic and reason.

"Considering the weather, the rapid news updates, not to mention the havoc and devastation of the last few days, I'd say we were lucky to get out of there alive!!!"

Candy knew he was right. Pete would find a way to get them out of this mess, he always did. It was getting dark as they approached the sign that read "YOU ARE NOW LEAVING CATLANTIS."

Pete breathed a sigh of relief; he knew that another episode in their lives was about to unfold.

He had been driving for a few hours and was keen to get as much distance between the Winnie and Catlantis, before stopping for a break.

The Kitty Katz had finished their dinner and were watching an episode of "Paws 4 Thought," a quiz show that was popular in Catlantis.

The laughter was infectious. Pete was glad of the solitude at the helm of the Winnebago. He was taking the opportunity to clear his head and plan where they would refuel for the remainder of the journey.

He found himself being mentally interrupted by thoughts of his political career. "Fifty miles more gang, then I'm pulling over for gas" Pete shouted. He heard one "Okay" and a lot of laughing.

Pete chuckled to himself. He was glad that they seemed to be taking the whole episode in their stride. With his thoughts, the stars, and the road markings to keep him company, the plan was to get as many miles under his belt as possible.

He found himself thinking about Candy, and how they first met. She was his high school sweetheart; it was love at first sight. After years of dating, she said "I do," and promised to be his walking catnip… forever.

Pete was still smiling at the memory of the day he beat Felix Schmeckel, the captain of the basketball team, to win a date with Candy.

Felix had a reputation for being a ladies' man, a smooth operator and a bit of a Catsanova. That would not stop Pete. One thing he refused to be beaten at was revision, homework, or a test.

Pete was a five-star, grade A, nerd. So, who knows what possessed Felix and made him think he could win a test, especially a spelling test, against "Professor Pete" as his friends nicknamed him.

It was to be a "ten-word challenge" the winner would get to take Candy on a date, and the loser would forever weep. Pete knew, he had this in the bag.

CHAPTER 4

As the Catlantis city lights faded into the rearview, the wheels of the Winnebago hummed along the highway, the hypnotic roar comforted and reassured Pete. The Katz family were safe, sound, and in the midst of yet another unplanned adventure.

The long drive in the Winnebago provides plenty of opportunities for bonding and conversations among the Katz family.

Pete talks fondly about meeting Candy and tells entertaining stories from his youth to the Kitty Katz. He good-naturedly handles them teasing about his old-school music tastes and off-key singing.

The family enjoys playing road trip games together, they also discuss plans, hopes, and concerns about starting a new life in strange surroundings. What they wish to find in their new surroundings is also a hot topic.

As the atmosphere becomes light-hearted, the twins, Kool & Ki-Ki, tease each other and bicker in the close quarters. They try to include Pete Jnr but he is in his own musical world, playing his "air guitar."

The moon hung in the ink-black sky, a silent observer of the Katz family's journey into the unknown. Pete's mind, however, was not only on the road ahead.

It was also navigating the uncharted territory of what lay ahead in Barkadia Bay. He glanced at Candy, who sat beside him, a silent source of strength and support.

The radio, playing a lively tune, kept the atmosphere upbeat in the cockpit of the Winnebago. Candy was still deep in meditation, her composure unwavering even in the face of uncertainty.

Pete Snr peered into the rearview mirror, catching glances of the Kitty Katz, each now absorbed in their own individual world.

Pete Jnr, with his headphones on, was listening to what he considered the latest "cool" tunes. Kiera had her nose buried in her phone, scrolling through social media updates, while Kyle was engaged in an intense online game.

Pete Snr decided to break the silence. "Hey, Junior, what's the latest tune you've got there?" he asked, raising his eyebrows.

Pete Jnr removed his headphones, revealing a cascade of unruly fur. "It's the new hit from Meow Mania. Catchy, huh?"

"More like scratchy," teased Kyle, a mischievous glint in his eye.

"Oh, come on, you two," Candy interjected without opening her eyes. "Let Junior enjoy his music."

Pete Jnr grinned and put his headphones back on, returning to his musical haven. The family continued their journey through the night.

At the helm of the Winnebago, Pete Snr gazes contemplatively out the window, reminiscing about his grandfather, "Whiskers," and the wise advice he gave Pete as a kitten.

Grandad Whiskers taught me so much growing up, he thought, integrity, honesty, and standing up for what's right. I sure could use his wisdom now, leading my family into this unknown. If only you were still with us Grandad, we would...

Pete's eyes grow heavy. Soon he drifts off to sleep at the wheel. The Winnebago swerves sharply!!!

CHAPTER 5

Candy grabs the wheel, stabilizing the vehicle.

Pete wakes with a shock as the Winnebago screeched to a halt. He had fallen asleep after driving all night.

"DAD, are you ok?" asked a concerned Junior.

"Yeah, I'm fine," Pete replied wearily. "Just a little tired."

Kiera took an eye off her phone for a moment. Kyle sat up, wide-eyed and alert, like a meerkat.

Candy handed Pete a thermos of coffee. "Here hon, this should help. Why don't you let me drive for a while?"

Pete readily agreed. As Candy took over driving duties, Pete settled into the passenger seat. The strong coffee was already working its magic.

CHAPTER 6

Pete looked up at the night sky, which was adorned with countless stars, and remembered the various constellations that he had been shown by his Grandfather Whiskers, who was a member of the Catlantis Astronomical Society.

In his new role as co-pilot, Pete checked the satellite navigation on the dashboard, he knew they were nearing a rest area where they could pause for the night.   Relief swept over him.

Meanwhile, Candy was enjoying being at the helm of the Winnebago, a position she hadn't held for a while.

She smiled to herself and thought, such clever creatures those humans are, as she looked at the cat's eyes on the highway and thought about the fantastic cat-inspired contribution her species had made to the world.

The atmosphere inside the vehicle was a mix of excitement, worry, and anticipation.

"Candy Girl," Pete said, wrapping his tail around his wife's, "Let's make a stop, there's a rest area a few miles away." Candy nods, her eyes gleaming with a hint of determination.

Moments later, Candy skilfully pulls into the cozy rest area, a refuge for tired travellers.

The family members stretched their legs and gathered outside, welcoming the cool night air.

The Kitty Katz were instantly drawn to a playground nearby, their laughter echoing through the quiet night.

Pete looked at Candy with a loving smile. "We're on another unplanned adventure, Candy Girl."

She nodded, returning the smile. "We'll get through it Pete. Katz can handle anything."

They high five, their paws meeting in the cool night air.

The rest area had a small convenience store where Pete bought snacks and drinks for the family. They gathered around a picnic table, sharing stories and reminiscing about their past adventures.

Meanwhile, Pete Jnr sat quietly gazing at the stars. Candy noticed his distant look and joined him. "What's on your mind Jnr?"

He hesitated before speaking. "I don't know Mom. It's just... things are going to be different now. I miss Catlantis. This emergency, moving to an unknown place, it's all a bit scary."

Candy put her paw around him and purred reassuringly. "The only thing permanent is change. Change is a part of life Jnr, Catlantis wasn't safe for us anymore. But no matter what happens, we're a family, and we'll always be there for each other."

As the night deepened, Pete gathered everyone for a group meditation session, just like they used to do in Catlantis. They sat in a circle, closed their eyes, and focused on their breathing.

Candy guided them through a calming meditation, once again bringing a sense of unity and peace to the Katz family.

CHAPTER 7

As the Winnebago rumbled down the deserted highway, the Katz family remained silent, each contemplating the uncertainty that lay ahead.

Kiera gazed pensively out the window at the dusty landscape passing by. Mile after empty mile, they hadn't passed a single car or even a building.

Then suddenly, Kiera bolted upright. "DAD STOP!!!" she cried, banging the glass.

Pete pumps the huge Winnebago brakes, slowing down the vehicle.

Before the Winnebago came to a complete stop, Kiera had, in a flash, bounded outside. Candy gracefully and speedily followed behind.

Slowly, they approached a young feline, slumped against a solitary tree, her haunted expression tore at Kiera's heart.

"Hi... I'm Kiera. This is my Mum. What's your name? Are you okay?"

The girl shivered despite the afternoon heat. "M-m-my name's Angora Kish," she whispered, fresh tears carving trails in the dust on her cheeks. "I'm trying to get to Barkadia Bay."

Horror dropped like a stone in Kiera's stomach. She knelt and offered her paw, which Angora grasped desperately, her paw trembling.

Candy embraced Angora tightly as if protecting her own lost babe.

"We'll look after you," she comforted, holding back tears as they helped limp Angora into the Winnebago.

Angora manages a small grateful smile.

As Pete jammed the gas pedal, Angora's story tumbled out amidst crippling sobs. She had briefly left her loving family relaxing after dinner, when the earth violently claimed them - swallowing Angora's entire world without warning.

Angora had nipped out to grab milk and some treats from the corner store, while her family relaxed after supper with merry laughter ringing melodiously through their cozy home.

But, on Angora's return….

"They were just gone!!! The house, Mom, Dad, my baby sister Tia. All I could find was this," her voice shaking, while holding on tight to a dusty teddy bear. "My sister's bear, Honey."

Angora dissolved into incoherent wailing.

The words hung heavily in the air. The Katz family sat paralyzed. Even rowdy Kyle and Junior were struck dumb, blinking back silent tears.

Candy whispers frantic prayers while clinging to Angora. Pete stares straight ahead, his jaw tight.

Kiera simply held Angora's hand - no words could soothe this pain.

She recognized the light in Angora's eyes had been robbed without reason. Pete vowed to help Angora find her family.

CHAPTER 8

The road unfolded ahead of them, winding through landscapes both familiar and unknown. Pete couldn't shake off the feeling that something significant awaited them.

As they approached the city limits, a billboard caught Pete's eye. "WELCOME TO BARKADIA BAY – Where Cats and Dogs Coexist."

The sight of this billboard brought a mixture of relief and curiosity.

Pete decided to explore potential neighbourhoods for their new home.

The family drove through charming streets lined with houses, parks, and stores. It was a stark contrast to the constant upheaval they faced in Catlantis.

Eventually, they found a cozy neighbourhood with friendly faces and a sense of community. Pete Jnr even made a few friends at the local skate park. Kool, Ki-Ki, and new addition Angora discovered a vibrant arts scene that piqued their interest.

Pete and Candy felt a sense of belonging in Barkadia Bay. They located a beautiful home on Barkadia Bay Boulevard with enough room for them all.

Over the next few months, the Katz family worked hard to rebuild their lives in Barkadia Bay.

Pete and Candy enrolled Pete Jnr, the twins and Angora in the local high school. Making new friends and joining after-school clubs helped them settle in.

Meanwhile, Pete searched relentlessly for employment. With his background in local politics, he hoped to land something in Barkadia Bay's city council.

Over a dinner of tuna casserole, the family reassures Angora and makes thoughtful plans to locate her missing relatives.

After many interviews, Pete finally got a call with a job offer. He had been selected as assistant to the Mayor of Barkadia Bay.

Pete gladly accepted.

On Pete's first day at city hall, the Mayor, Mr. Shepherd, a friendly border collie, greeted him. "Welcome aboard, Pete! We're lucky to have someone with your qualifications and experience on our team," the sheepdog said. "Thank you, Sir," Pete said with an appreciative tone.

He knew all eyes were on him. Being the first feline to have a position in the history of the Barkadia Bay city council, which was over six hundred years old, was a great accomplishment. Pete was honoured. For the first time since leaving Catlantis, he felt a sense of purpose.

Meanwhile, Candy managed to secure a storefront on Barkadia Bay Lane to open a beauty salon. Her business took off quickly, thanks to the high-end professional service and rave reviews.

Before long, her clientele included celebrities and some of the most fashionable ladies in town, both cats and dogs alike.

With her thriving beauty business, she joined forces with other feline and canine mompreneurs in the city.

The Katz family were finally getting back on their paws. The future was looking bright.

CHAPTER 9

The scent of cedarwood and red amber kissed the air. Candy sat in the lotus position and meditated. It was the only 'me time,' that she could carve out of her busy schedule these days.

Candy's beauty salon had gone from strength to strength. The thriving business became a symbol of relaxation and pampering in Barkadia Bay.

Her clients, both cats and dogs, appreciated the beauty techniques and treatments, creating a common bond between the two species.

Her next client was due after lunch, one of her regulars, Mrs Silverstein. The Silversteins had left Catlantis at the same time as the Katz family.

They had known each other for many years and were in the same social circles. Candy knew she would be able to catch up on all the "news."

She was, however, a little concerned about Pete Jnr who seemed to be behaving out of character.

CHAPTER 10

A few months had passed. Pete, who was very accomplished, settled nicely into the job at city hall, almost effortlessly. His friends had always joked that if he threw his C.V. into the air, it would turn into a halo.

He was making great progress towards drafting the "Catlantis Rescue Program," to search for any survivors. His proposals were set to be reviewed in an upcoming council meeting.

Meanwhile, as junior year midterms approached, straight-A student Kiera Katz was laser-focused on maintaining her stellar GPA.

Kyle and his garage band buddies were busy preparing for Barkadia Bay High's annual battle of the bands.

Angora, who was settling down and getting used to the major changes she had experienced, was taking the Barkadia Bay gymnastics scene by storm.

One evening over dinner, talk turned to Junior. Recently, he had been staying out late without explanation. His parents were growing concerned about the company he was keeping.

"What have you been up to after school, son?" Pete gently prodded.

"Just hanging out with some friends," Junior replied evasively between bites of salmon steaks.

Candy and Pete exchanged a worried glance but didn't press further.

They hoped Junior would confide in them when he was ready. For now, he was still getting good grades, so his personal life was not an urgent issue…. yet.

Little did they know what trouble was brewing right under their noses...

CHAPTER 11

In the heart of Barkadia Bay, where the sun painted the sky with hues of warmth, Angora sat on the Katz family's porch, savouring the breeze.

She traced her paw along the intricate patterns of the welcome mat, a tangible reminder of the newfound home she had discovered with the Katz family.

The Katz family, understanding Angora's journey, had made special efforts to integrate her into their lives. Pete Katz Snr would often share tales from Catlantis, bonding over shared memories of a homeland they both missed. The Kitty Katz—Kiera, Kyle, and Junior—embraced Angora as if she had always been a part of their lives.

Candy, with her therapeutic touch, organized meditation sessions for the entire family, creating a serene space where unity thrived.

Angora discovered a sense of belonging she hadn't known before. The communal spirit of the city, and the genuine friendships she forged with both cats and dogs, had melted away the walls she'd built around herself.

Her days were now filled with shared laughter, playful banter, and moments of pure youthful feline fun.

It wasn't just the Katz family who embraced Angora, the entire neighbourhood had rallied around her. They had thrown a "Welcome Angora" party, where cats and dogs alike exchanged stories and celebrated their newfound unity. Angora's radiant smile became a symbol of the transformative power of acceptance.

One evening, as the sun dipped below the horizon, the Katz family and Angora gathered on the rooftop of their home.

With the twinkling lights of Barkadia Bay spread before them, Pete Katz Snr proposed a toast, "To Angora, who taught us that our hearts are bigger when we welcome others into them."

Amidst the clinking of glasses and the symphony of purrs and meows, Angora felt a flow of heartwarming emotions – gratitude, joy, and an overwhelming sense of belonging.

CHAPTER 12

Pete Katz Snr heaved a sigh of relief as he arrived home after a long, challenging day at city hall.

As he looked towards the house, he noticed a delicate figure curled up near the doorstep. It was Angora, the once-lonely cat who had become an integral part of their lives. Her eyes once filled with trepidation, now mirrored a mixture of sadness and hope.

"Angora, sweetheart, what are you doing out here?" Pete's voice, a soothing melody, reached her ears. She looked up, her gaze meeting his with a vulnerability that tugged at his heartstrings.

Pete sat beside her. Angora's soft fur pressed against his hand as she leaned into his comforting presence.

The evening was quiet, cradling their shared silence, each heartbeat resonating with the weight of their collective experiences.

"I miss them, Uncle Pete," Angora whispered, her voice barely audible. "My family, my friends—Catlantis, it all feels like a distant dream."

Pete felt a pang of empathy, a shared ache. He understood the ache of loss, the yearning for a place that once felt like home. In that moment, he saw Angora not just as a cat but as a soul seeking solace.

"We'll find them, Angora," Pete said, his voice carrying a promise laced with determination. "I can't stand the thought of anyone getting left behind. There's hope sweetheart."

Angora's eyes, a tapestry of emotions, lit up with a flicker of optimism. Pete continued, "You're not alone in this, Angora. We're a family, and we take care of our own. We'll face whatever comes our way."

As Pete spoke those words, a sense of unity enveloped them. Angora, once a solitary figure in a world turned upside down, now found comfort in the warmth of Pete's assurance.

The porch, once a symbol of transition, became a sanctuary of shared passion and purpose.

CHAPTER 13

The next day, Pete and the rest of the household were sure to get home early for dinner.

Candy was making her famous seafood medley pie, a recipe that was sacred in the Katz household.

Once they were all seated and the smell of the pie was wafting around the dinner table, Pete cleared his throat. "Before we eat this beautiful seafood medley pie, thank you Candy, I have some news. Which do you want first, the good news or the bad news?"

"The bad news" Kiera quickly meowed, before anyone else could even purr. "Well, the bad news is…. there is no good news." Pete said with a bleak tone. "So, what's the good news?" Kiera said, slightly puzzled, her brow furrowed. "The good news is …… there's no bad news either." He said smiling. They all laughed. Kiera smiled and rolled her eyes.

Pete Snr was in a good mood, and that always brought out the comedian in him. His proposals had been well received at city hall. "Seriously though …" Pete started "My proposals for the Catlantis Rescue Program have been voted on, and are set to receive immediate funding."

"That's brilliant Hon," said Candy, her voice full of pride that Pete was able to affect such a positive action. "Well done, Dad," "Great work Dad," "Nice going Dad," said the other voices.

Angora sat with a smile on her lips and a tear in her eye, and whispered, her voice cracking with emotion "Thank you, Uncle Pete."

Kiera leaned over and gave Angora, who was sitting next to her, a comforting hug.

"That's not all" continued Pete. Now, they all became even more interested, and hung on his every word, anticipating what was to follow the big news they had just heard……

CHAPTER 14

Pete's political career in Barkadia Bay took an unexpected turn. He felt a genuine connection with the locals and a shared vision for a more harmonious coexistence between canines and felines.

Encouraged by the positive response from the community and the warmth they had all experienced since arriving, he decided to run for a position as ……….

Pete cleared his throat. "As the current Mayor's tenure is reaching full term, I've decided to run for office. Mayor, to be precise."

The revelation was met with a symphony of reactions. Angora clapped. Junior Katz looked up wide-eyed. Kyle raised an eyebrow, giving a subtle nod of approval.

Kiera, however, broke the silence with a burst of laughter. "Dad, are you kitten me right meow? Mayor? In a town run by dogs!!!"

Pete grinned, embracing the feline pun. "Yes, Kiera. I've always believed in the power of change. And sometimes, you must be the cat to catch the mouse."

Candy leaned in, whispering, "Pete, this is purr-plexing news. When did you decide this?"

Pete winked at her. "Candy Girl, sometimes life throws you a curveball, and you've got to swing back. Besides, it's not just about us anymore. It's about cats and dogs living side by side, without the threat of a pending emergency hanging over their heads.”

“Can we eat now? I’m starving” asked a hungry Kyle.

“Y’all eat up and enjoy” smiled Candy, excited at the carnival of flavours that awaited them.

CHAPTER 15

Junior Katz waited anxiously by the lockers after the final bell, checking his phone compulsively. He was supposed to meet Felix and the boys to hang out.

Finally, Felix, Tom & Titus – a group of shady alley cats – sauntered into view. "Wassup Katz," Felix greeted Junior with an elaborate pawshake. "You ready to have some fun?"

Junior nodded nervously. He wasn't entirely comfortable with Felix and his friends, but he was desperate to impress them and to be considered "cool."

Felix led the group towards the parking lot behind the Fish & Bone Cafe. "You ready for the ride of your life Katz?" He teased as he opened the door of an old sedan.

Junior watched wide-eyed as Felix started the engine. "Hop in boys, we're going for a ride!" Felix cackled. Against his better judgement, Pete Jnr got in.

"I didn't know you had a sedan, Felix." Pete Jnr said, sounding impressed.

"I borrowed it from a friend, Katz." Felix said smiling. Tom and Titus laughed. Pete Jnr failed to see what was so funny.

Felix drove wildly through the streets. Panicked, Junior asked to be let out after a few blocks. This was getting out of hand fast! "Don't worry about it, you'll be fine." Felix reassured.

Just then, sirens sounded and lights flashed behind them. Felix mumbled something and pushed down harder on the gas pedal. "Hold on tight!"

CHAPTER 16

Felix raced towards the old factory district, trying to lose the cop car on their tail. Pete Jnr clutched his seat, ears pressed flat. "How did I get myself into this mess?" he thought.

Suddenly, Felix took a sharp turn and one of the car's back tires blew out. They careered across the road and crashed nose-first into a set of trash cans.

A cloud of dust and smoke filled the air. Junior coughed. He was stunned but thankfully unharmed. Then, three doors opened at once. Felix, Tom, and Titus jumped out of the sedan and over a wall, effortlessly. They could be heard meowing and laughing as they ran away.

Meanwhile, before Pete Jnr could even open the door, Officer Growl, a heavy-set rottweiler, had him cornered. "Well, well, well, who do we have here then, in this stolen car?" he snarled.

Junior gulped nervously while trembling uncontrollably.

CHAPTER 17

Back at the Katz home, the phone rang. Candy answered – it was Officer Growl.

She sunk onto the couch in shock, after Officer Growl explained what had happened. How could her precious Junior get mixed up in something so dangerous?

Pete came home soon after to comfort his distraught wife. "Don't worry honey. We'll get to the bottom of this," he assured her.

Later at the station, a shame-faced Junior recounted the whole story. Pete's heart broke, seeing his son wrapped up in Felix's hoodlum crew.

Since Junior's record was clean, he got off with a stern warning. On the ride home, Pete had a long talk with his son about peer pressure, self-respect, embracing his uniqueness and making better choices.

Junior, who was glad to be going home in one piece, took his dad's wise words to heart. He knew it was time to get out of Felix's toxic circle for good.

CHAPTER 18

Campaigning became a family affair. The Katz organized rallies, participated in parades, and even hosted a "Paws for Peace" event that brought together felines and canines.

Posters featuring a charismatic cat with the slogan "KATZ KAN!!!" popped up on every doghouse and scratching post. Pete's voice echoed through the city as he delivered speeches, promising unity and equality for cats and dogs.

The mayoral journey, however, was not without its challenges. Pete found himself in a heated televised debate, facing off against three other candidates.

Fiery pit bull, Rex Barkington-Bones, a seasoned and articulate politician, who was currently leading in the polls. Wilfred Woofson, an accomplished leonberger, who pledged to uphold law & order, and sniff out corruption in the town, and Coco Bowwowski, the afghan hound with graceful allure, who promised to bring a touch of elegance, wisdom, and optimism to the office of mayor.

The air crackled with tension as they sparred over policies and visions for Barkadia Bay.

However, Pete's sincerity and the heartfelt support from the community began to shift the tide.

One particularly intense exchange came from Coco Bowwowski, who challenged Pete. "What makes you think a cat can bring about change? We've always been in charge."

Pete, ever the diplomat, responded like a cool cat, "Well, Coco, sometimes it takes a Katz perspective to see the bigger picture. Let's build a world of unity and equality where every paw counts."

During the debate, Rex snarled, "What does a cat know about leading a city? You spend your time chasing mice and sleeping, not solving real issues."

Pete maintained his composure, responding with a twinkle in his eye, "Well, Rex, sometimes you need a cat's intuition to catch the subtle issues that may slip past a dog's nose."

The audience erupted into laughter, and the tension dissolved. Pete's wit and charm had won over the crowd, earning him not just votes but a nickname—Pete the Purr-suader.

After the debate, Pete was approached by a reporter. The charming saluki named Luna Tailstein had been sceptical about a cat running for mayor in a town run by canines. Luna was intrigued by Pete.

"Pete Katz, you've achieved something remarkable here. How did you manage to survive such a dog fight?"

With a knowing smile, Pete replied, "Luna, it's all about finding common ground, appreciating our differences, and realizing that we're all part of this grand tapestry of life. Besides, a good joke and a friendly purr can go a long way." They both laughed.

CHAPTER 19

A few weeks later, strange things started happening around Barkadia Bay. Manhole covers disappeared overnight. Cars got stuck in odd holes that seemingly appeared out of nowhere.

Pete soon noticed a worrying pattern.

One morning, Junior burst into his dad's home office looking alarmed. "Dad, you gotta come with me, now!"

Pete followed his son out to the backyard where the earth had split open, revealing a gaping sinkhole. Pete's blood ran cold. His worst fears had come true – the sinkholes were back in their lives.

He realized then why contact had been lost with Catlantis. The land must have become so plagued with tunnels that it collapsed in on itself. Pete shuddered at the thought.

After investigating, Pete learned that questionable real estate deals had allowed the overdevelopment of fragile land in the Barkadia Bay region. This was the culprit behind the new sinkholes threatening families' homes and safety.

Pete brought his findings to Mayor Shepherd. "We need to stop approvals for new construction right away until the land can be stabilized sir," he urged.

Shepherd shook his head. "I can't do that Pete. It would tank our whole local economy; construction contracts are already in place. Many corporations are planning to set up businesses in Barkadia Bay."

"But the foundations are not safe sir. We can't put profits before the safety of the residents" Pete protested.

"I'm sorry Katz, It's, it's, it's out of my paws." Said the Mayor, sounding like a dog on a leash that was being controlled.

Pete left the office fuming. Politics and money were being put before life and safety. Drastic action was needed to force reform and protect Barkadia Bay residents.

Like his favourite TV detective, Catlumbo, Pete could smell a rat.

CHAPTER 20

The door to the Katz household swung open, Pete Katz Snr entered with the weariness of a cat who had just faced a thousand dogs. His shoulders slouched under the invisible burden of being the first and only feline to work at Barkadia Bay's city hall. The strains of a challenging day lingered on his whiskers, and uncertainty cast shadows over his usually confident eyes.

Candy, with her empathetic feline grace, sensed Pete's unease. She greeted him with a soft purr, brushing her cheek against his. "Rough day at the office, my love?" she inquired, her eyes reflecting concern.

Pete sighed, "It feels like I'm climbing a mountain covered in dog fur, Candy. The polls are still against me, and being the only cat at city hall is tougher than I thought."

Candy led him to the living room, where the aroma of a home-cooked meal wafted from the kitchen. "Sit, Pete. You've earned a moment's rest." She poured him a cup of chamomile tea, knowing its calming effects would help soothe his frazzled nerves.

As Pete took a sip, he looked into Candy's eyes, searching for solace. "I'm starting to doubt if I can win this election. Maybe I'm pushing too hard for unity and equality between the species. The city might not be ready for a feline mayor."

Candy gently touched his paw, her voice filled with unwavering support. "Pete, remember why you started this journey. You wanted to bring harmony between our feline and canine friends. It's not just about being a mayor; it's about creating a better world for everyone."

Pete nodded, grateful for Candy's wisdom. "You're right, Candy. But sometimes, it feels like I'm clawing at a brick wall."

Candy smiled. "Dinner will be ready in half an hour. Before that, why don't you take some time to meditate? Clear your mind. You've always found your way when you've had a moment of quiet reflection."

Seeing the genuine concern in Candy's eyes, Pete decided to follow her advice. He found a quiet spot in their cozy home, closed his eyes, and focused on his breath. The rhythm of inhaling and exhaling became a refuge from the chaos outside.

As Pete delved into meditation, his mind began to settle. In the stillness, he felt a familiar presence—a whisper from his grandfather, Whiskers.

The old cat's voice echoed, "Pete, my boy, you're on the right path. Embrace the challenges, for they shape the leader within. Remember, unity is not a sprint; it's a marathon."

Whiskers continued, "Hear me well Pete, the rift between the two species traces back generations, but the root lies with questionable land rights and deals that left cats segregated to unsafe grounds riddled with sinkholes! Political grievances festered as the divide grew...but you now have the power to bridge this gap by proposing secure infrastructure standards. There is a grander destiny here Peter...walk in truth and light. The time has come for cats and dogs to unite at last!"

Gasping, Pete is yanked back to wakefulness! Candy hovers over him looking worried. Pete pants heavily trying to gather his thoughts...

Opening his eyes, Pete felt a renewed sense of purpose. Candy was right; he couldn't let doubt overshadow his dreams. He rejoined Candy in the kitchen, where the aroma of a hearty meal awaited them.

Over dinner, Candy listened to Pete share his aspirations, his doubts, and the echoes of his grandfather's wisdom which he experienced during meditation. She assured him. "You're not just running for mayor; you're running for a cause. And no matter what the polls say, you've already made a difference in Barkadia Bay."

Pete smiled, feeling the warmth of Candy's support. In that moment, he understood that leadership wasn't about instant victories but a journey of perseverance, compassion, and the unwavering belief that unity was achievable.

The Katz family gathered around the dinner table, laughter and love filled the air. The challenges ahead seemed less daunting, knowing that they faced them together.

As the evening unfolded, Pete found solace not only in the comforting embrace of his family but in the realization that the path to unity, though rocky, was worth every step.

CHAPTER 21

Pete called an emergency town hall meeting and invited the press. He presented strong evidence of the sinkhole emergency caused by rampant overdevelopment. Livid families echoed Pete's demand to stop all new construction permits.

When Mayor Shepherd gave vague excuses, the crowd's anger boiled over, as they called for his immediate resignation. Pete saw this as a tipping point not just locally, but globally.

He made an impassioned speech: "The real estate corruption behind these environmental disasters only perpetuates conflict between cats and dogs. It ends today with my Cats and Dogs Sinkhole Safety and Cooperation Act!"

The room erupted into applause. Pete's land reform bill gained such rapid popular support that Shepherd and the council had no choice but to pass it into urgent law.

Construction was halted on dangerous land. New foundations were shored up. Families like Pete's could now rest easy in their homes, thanks to his Cats and Dogs Sinkhole Safety and Cooperation Act, which the Barkadia Bay Gazette celebrated on their front page.

Pete Katz became an ambassador for the cause, traveling to different cities, attending conferences, and inspiring others to embrace the spirit of cooperation.

CHAPTER 22

At the next quarterly Inter-Species Relations summit, Pete brought global leaders together to amend building codes everywhere.

This was a big occasion for Pete Katz. He had come a long way. His passion outweighed his nervousness.

Pete stood at the podium, looking out over the sea of expectant faces in the grand hall.

Diplomats and dignitaries from around the world awaited his address at this urgent Global Accord meeting.

After a discreet cough, Pete began. "Esteemed guests, we gather today with renewed hope, after the miraculous discovery of Catlantis survivors in underground bunkers. However, this revelation also carries sombre lessons."

Pete met Candy's glistening eyes. "When those early warning signs appeared in our hometown, we scarcely imagined the vast suffering beneath our paws. Had more cats and dogs cooperated then, perhaps we could have prevented Catlantis's catastrophic fate."

His voice quivered. "As one who barely escaped that collapse with my family, I carry immense regret and sorrow over the uncounted lost souls we left behind."

The hall grew hushed. Pete steadied himself before continuing. "We cannot change the past, but we can shape the future. Let the scarred terrain of Catlantis stand forever protected, reminding all the senseless peril that comes when our species clash."

Applause erupted. Pete raised a paw for silence. "The Salvation of Catlantis Survivors Act will relocate all remaining families, but our duty extends beyond mere evacuation."

Pete unveiled an elaborate map. "Behold, my proposal for an interspecies development - New Catlantis. This model community will rise adjacent to the memorial grounds. Here, cats and dogs shall build side-by-side to demonstrate eternal harmony."

He continued. "We must have standards to construct only on stable land, both for safety and environmental reasons; we must forgo opportunities to enrich ourselves at the expense of our shared home.

Sinkholes may seem like a localized issue, but they symbolise the fractures in our collective responsibility. Our feline and canine citizens have endured enough displacement due to these treacherous pits.

Today, I implore global leaders to unite for a fundamental change. Let us not allow our homes to crumble beneath our feet. Both literally and metaphorically.

The Katz family, along with countless others, has faced the upheaval caused by these sinkholes.

We cannot turn a blind eye to the devastating consequences. It's time to put aside differences, be they feline or canine, and forge a pact for the well-being of our world.

I propose an international summit, where we draft the "Unity Accord"- a commitment to responsible construction, environmental stewardship, and solidarity among all creatures.

Together, we can ensure a stable future for every family, regardless of their species. Let us build bridges, not create sinkholes, and pave the way for a world where unity triumphs over discord. The time for action is now."

Excited murmurs filled the room. Council Leader Winston, a rotund bulldog, stood first in ovation. "Brilliant, Katz! The world sorely needs your visionary leadership on the Global Stage!"

This was followed by a standing ovation. The room filled with leaders from various species, resonated with the harmony of applause.

It wasn't just the words; it was the impassioned plea for unity that struck a chord. As Pete descended from the podium, he felt a wave of support and camaraderie from those who were once sceptical.

At that moment, Pete knew the seed of change had been planted. The journey ahead would be challenging, but the collective applause echoed a shared commitment to building a future where sinkholes were mere memories and unity triumphed over discord.

After much negotiation, the tense summit concluded with the landmark "Global Accord for Construction Standards" which the press dubbed the "Pete's Treaty."

CHAPTER 23

As Pete and Candy watched highlights of the summit's success on the TV at home, relief washed over them. "You did a wonderful thing for cats everywhere, hon." Candy purred with pride. Pete pulled her into an embrace.

"I just wish this treaty could have come sooner. Maybe we could have prevented the loss of Catlantis," he lamented.

"Don't mourn what's past. Just look now - Kitty Katz worldwide will have you to thank!" Candy nodded at the twins Kyle and Kiera who were actively monitoring their social feeds.

"Woah, Dad - you're trending!" Kyle exclaimed. "Look at all the memes and hashtags!" True enough, #PetesTreaty and #PeteForPresident were gathering steam rapidly online, after his address at the summit went viral.

Pete rubbed his neck self-consciously. "It's not about fame. I'm just trying to make the world safer."

Just then, Junior entered the room, smiling brighter than he had in ages. "You're a hero Dad! And hey...can I ask you something?"

Pete studied his son. Junior seemed to have gained maturity recently. "Sure son, what is it?"

"Well, after everything that happened with the sinkholes and seeing you stand up for what's right...It inspired me. I want to run for Class President on making schools environmentally sustainable!" Junior explained eagerly.

Pride surged in Pete's heart hearing Junior take such an impassioned stance. He pulled Junior into a fatherly hug. "I'm so proud of you son!"

CHAPTER 24

At that moment, the TV summit highlights were interrupted. "Breaking News" the voice said, with a serious tone.

The broadcaster continues...... "In a shocking turn of events, Rex Barkington-Bones, the political figure and mayoral candidate, is under intense scrutiny.

An exhaustive investigation has exposed back door deals between the charismatic pit bull and land developers, resulting in rampant overdevelopment, the root cause of the catastrophic sinkholes plaguing Barkadia Bay.

The "Permits for Pay" scandal has sent shockwaves through the community, shattering the trust once placed in Barkington-Bones. In a press conference, a furious Barkington-Bones denies any wrongdoing. He asserts his innocence, labelling the accusations as baseless attempts to tarnish his reputation."

The air in the Katz household grew heavy with disbelief as news of the Barkington-Bones scandal echoed through the living room.

Pete Katz, who had been tirelessly campaigning against his canine opponents, found himself caught in a whirlwind of surprise and contemplation.

The family exchanged glances, their feline eyes reflecting a mix of shock and uncertainty.

Candy Katz, sensing the weight of the revelation, placed a comforting paw on Pete's shoulder.

The once-imposing figure of Barkington-Bones, now tainted by allegations, had injected an unexpected twist into the mayoral race.

Pete felt a surge of mixed emotions – surprised at the revelation and a newfound determination to bring forth change.

The Kitty Katz, overhearing the hushed conversations, exchanged bewildered looks. The unfolding scandal had disrupted the already tense political landscape of Barkadia Bay.

CHAPTER 25

The day of the election was upon them, and a blend of excitement and nervous energy filled the Katz household. With Pete's growing popularity and the "Permits for Pay" scandal buzzing around Barkadia Bay, he started to rise in the polls.

Pete Snr, with a mix of nerves and determination, cast his vote early in the morning.

Barkadia Bay was alight with anticipation. The Katz family became the heartbeat of the city, their journey from sinkholes to city hall capturing the imagination of every resident.

Supporters were busy distributing Katz-themed treats to voters, each treat carrying a message of unity and equality. Pete, accompanied by Candy, stood in front of their campaign headquarters, a unity flag billowing in the breeze.

Kiera and Angora had organized a flash mob of dancing cats and dogs in the city square. While Kyle, with his phone in hand, was live-streaming the atmosphere.

As the votes were tallied, the air became charged with anticipation.

The Kitty Katz huddled together; their eyes glued to the news coverage. Pete paced nervously, his tail twitching with each passing moment.

The announcement echoed through the city. "And the new mayor of Barkadia Bay is...... Pete Katz!" Candy, with tears of happiness in her eyes, whispered to Pete Snr, "You did it, my love."

To their shock, Pete won by a huge margin, thanks to the cat vote which turned out in droves to support him. Ecstatic, the family embraced amid camera flashes.

The meows and barks that erupted from the crowd were deafening. Pete, with tears of joy, embraced Candy. The Kitty Katz surged forward, engulfing their parents in a furry group hug.

Pete, now Mayor Pete Katz, took to the stage, his voice resonating with gratitude. As Pete gave his victory speech, he made eye contact with Candy.

He knew he couldn't have done any of this without her endless love and support. She had encouraged him since the days of junior high spelling bees up through to the world stage.

With Candy by his side, Pete felt like he could achieve anything – and reshape history for the better.

"Barkadia Bay, today is not just a victory for me but a triumph for unity and equality. Together, we'll turn problems into challenges and challenges into opportunities. Katz Kan!!!, and together, we shall."

He continued. "I would like to take this opportunity to honour and welcome all the Catlantis survivors who are celebrating with us, in particular, the Kish family.

During a rescue mission to the ruins of Catlantis, an unbelievable discovery was made – a secret underground bunker sheltering survivors after all this time…" The crowd erupted into rapturous applause.

The Kish family were the parents of Angora. She had finally been reunited with her Mum, Dad, and baby sister Tia. The two families celebrated Pete's accomplishments.

The merriment continued, the city was alive with a harmonious blend of meows and barks, a testament to the newfound unity forged by the Katz family.

As fireworks painted the sky, Pete glanced at his family, knowing that this was just the beginning of their extraordinary journey in Barkadia Bay.

The tale of the Katz family, from sinkholes to city hall, had become a feline fairy tale, a story of courage, tenacity, and the purr-suit of a better world.

CHAPTER 26

Fellow mayoral candidates Coco Bowwowski and Wilfred Woofson congratulated Pete on becoming the first feline mayor in the history of Barkadia Bay.

They toasted to his success with a rare vintage Catnip Champagne as they posed for the press photographers.

However, one prominent figure was conspicuously absent from the jubilant celebrations.

CHAPTER 27

Meanwhile, in the affluent suburb of Wagsley, a picturesque town just outside of Barkadia Bay, a disgraced and humiliated Rex Barkington-Bones sat alone in his dimly lit study.

Rex sat at a palatial oak desk, on an oxblood-coloured leather chair, contemplating his next move. "I must clear my name. Why couldn't they understand that I was intending to boost the economy? More developments mean more businesses moving into Barkadia Bay, which means more jobs for the locals, and a boost to the economy" he thought.

He continued. "I may be a bit brash and hot-headed, but I always get the job done. I am a doer, not a talker!!!" His paw slammed against the oak desk. Anger bubbling up inside of him.

Rex powered on the laptop which sat in front of him. A blank screen stared back. The cursor flashed invitingly.

He took a sip from the crystal glass which sat on his desk, then began typing….

"Dogs Do – A Dog's Perspective. By Rex Barkington Bones"

"It all began when I was a pup in Kennelton. We were a family of eight with barely a bone between us, or a garden to bury it in…

THE END